**Marmot**

**Magpie**

**Blackbird**

**Crow**

**Hare**

**Dormouse**

**Hamster**

**Woodpecker**

**Bumblebees**

**Mole**

**Rabbit**

**Cricket**

**Ants**

**Owl**

**Weasel**

Hello,

Let me introduce myself. I'm Hedgehog,
one of the woodland folk – that's
my paw mark at the bottom of the page!
   Read all about our adventures
and get to know the world we live in.
We have a Spring Party, and
a pea pod competition, we build a
swimming pool, we're invited to
Blackbirds' Wedding, and we make a
boat out of a giant clog!
   But best of all, whatever we do,
we always have a wonderful time.

*Hedgehog*

Published in the United States of America by
Rand McNally & Company, 1984
© 1983 Piero Dami Editore, Italy
All rights reserved
Printed in Italy  G.E.P.  -  Cremona

ISBN O 528-82561-5

Library of Congress Catalog Card No. 84-60934

# Meet The Woodland Folk

Tony Wolf

**Rand McNally & Company**

Chicago · New York · San Francisco

# The Spring Party

Ah! The Spring Party! None of the woodland folk want to miss that!

The Spring Party, with Black Rat conducting "The Bumblebee, Cricket and Grasshopper Orchestra" under a cloudless starry sky, and a barrel full to the brim with sweet raspberry syrup!

Miss this party? Not likely!

The party starts, however, with a loud "OUCH!" that echoes all over the wood.

"Whatever's happened?" Tortoise asks Crow.

"What do you think it is?" Crow replies. "Hedgehog has hammered his paw nailing up the notice, just like he does every year!"

Which is exactly what did happen. Nobody pays much attention to it now. Not even Hedgehog himself.

**"Ouch! That hurt!"**

All the woodland folk have come to the party. But this year there's a stranger: a frog. Nobody knows who he is, where he's come from or where he's going, but he's made welcome all the same. Shrew says to him:

"You see, now that the band has played the Pancake Song, the dancing starts."

"What's a pancake got to do with your party?" asks the frog.

"I don't know. Nobody knows! It's just a song we like!"

That, of course, is the secret of the woodland dwellers. Never ask too many questions. Life is difficult enough as it is. Badger, for example, points out on the calendar that the first day of Spring is tomorrow, not today. Do you know what Bear Cub and Fox say to him? "Dear Badger, you can throw a party any day!"

Now they've started to dance. Frog has asked Magpie to dance.

"Oh, thank you. I was so afraid Hedgehog was going to ask me. Can you imagine what it would be like with all those prickles!"

Squirrel hands round the raspberry drink, Water Rat offers the cakes, and all around there's a great hustle and bustle and much chattering. The band is playing and everyone is happy.

Well, to tell the truth, there is one scowling face! It's Crow's. His bowler

hat is crammed over his eyes and his wings are folded behind his back. He feels things are not going as they should.

"Craaw! Craaw! I say and say again, Craaw! These parties are silly!" he grumbles. "Why not have a summer party or a mid-autumn one? I don't like it. I'm not enjoying myself! I should have stayed at home! Here, you two!" he exclaims, turning to Beaver and Marmot. "What are you laughing at?"

"Ha! Ha! Ha! . . . Who, us? We're . . . Ha! Ha! Ha! . . . We're not laughing at all!"

They laugh so much their sides ache, and do you know why? Because Beaver had just asked Marmot, "Why does Crow never take off his bowler hat?"

"Don't you know?" Marmot had replied. "He's got a bald head!"

Poor old grumpy Crow, with his bald head! He complains he's bored at the party, but really he's having the time of his life. And when the party's over, and everyone has gone to bed in their nests and dens, tired, happy and contented, there he is, clearing up and taking away the rubbish. And as he does this, he mutters to himself:

"What fun the Spring Party is! I have a marvelous time! But, Craaw! Craaw! I say and repeat Craaw! The wood must be all clean and tidy for tomorrow! Otherwise, what would the flowers say!"

**And when the party's over,**
**Crow takes all the rubbish away in his garbage can.**

# The Pea Pod Competition

Peas! The two Hedgehog brothers love them. They rise early in the morning, when the birds are still fast asleep and the wood is silent and bathed in dew, and go to search for peas. Maybe they'll even stay out till dusk, but when they do come home, they have huge loads of green pods on their backs.

What a joy it is to split them open in the evening! The pods pop with a loud crack and the smell of fresh peas floats into the air!

"Mmmm! What a lovely smell! I'd love to gobble them all!" sighs one of the brothers, but the other, the wiser one, shakes his head:

"No, they're going into the barrels for salting."

"Just one or two! Please!"

"No! We have to think of winter, when there aren't any fresh vegetables."

As they work at filling the barrels, one of them says:

"Do you know, it's a shame to throw away the pods."

"Yes it is, but what can we do with them? You can't eat them!"

"Well, I'm sure they can be used for something. Look! Why don't we hold a competition? The person that suggests the best use for pea pods will be the winner of . . . Yes! Of a barrel of salted peas!"

The news spreads quickly and the next day everyone arrives with plenty of ideas. Frog says:

"We could paint a crest on each pod and have a canoe race."

Cricket says, "I suggest the pods be slung between two branches and used as hammocks! What a lovely snooze I could have!"

Ladybird suggests that a pea pod filled with water would make a bathtub.

Spider says, "I'd use them as fly-traps," but the others are horrified at the idea and tell him so. Spider goes off into a corner, in a huff.

"Why not use the pod as a cradle?" say the three Mouse Sisters, all speaking at once as usual.

**"What a lovely smell!
I bet they're delicious!"**

9

There's certainly no lack of ideas, and a discussion is still going on when up dashes Squirrel.

"Listen, folks!" he squeals. "Come and see what the Ants are doing!"

They all rush off to the stream. And when they get there, they stare in amazement.

For the Ants have lashed the pea pods together in pairs, like boats, and anchored them to the bottom of the stream (well, Frog did that, actually). Then they laid long sturdy stems of grass, all trimmed to the same length, across the pairs of pods. This was hard work and dangerous too, for they ran the risk of falling into the water. However, a rescue squad was standing by, armed with a life belt.

An hour or two later, a bridge was spanning the stream. Now, folk will no longer have to cross by the stepping stones, and get their feet wet.

"This is a splendid piece of work!" Beaver exclaims, and he knows a thing or two about building bridges because it's his job.

Frog says, "Dear Misses Mouse, would you like to cross first? Would you like to declare the bridge open?"

The three sisters ask hesitantly, "Um . . . declare . . . the bridge open?"

"Don't be alarmed! It's perfectly safe. This bridge could take an elephant! A very tiny elephant, of course."

"Come on! Come on!" urge the Hedgehogs.

So the three little Mouse Sisters pluck up courage and timidly set foot on the bridge. But they soon feel quite brave and walk firmly across, while the Ants clap and shout, "Hooray."

Everyone agrees that the Ants have won. So, with great pomp and ceremony they are awarded the prize for the best use of pea pods.

But Frog hasn't finished yet.

"I don't care about the prize," he says. "Anyway, I loathe salted peas. And now," he mutters, as he reaches for his paints and brush, "I'll paint a crest on the remaining pods . . . and here's to canoe racing on the stream!"

**Will the canoes Frog is painting really float?**
**It's just as well he's a good swimmer!**

11

# The Blackbirds' Wedding

Clink! Clink! Clink-clonk!

The woodland folk wake from sleep, blink their eyes, raise their heads and listen.

Clink! Clonk! Clink! Clink!

What is going on? Who is making that noise? A wakey-wakey call like this had never before been heard in the wood!

"Not to worry," says Crow, "I'll go and have a look."

He flies off the nest and flaps about till he hears that the sound is coming from a clump of bamboo. So he perches on a branch and peers down.

"Craaw! Craaw! I say and repeat, Craaw! It's Hare that is making the din! Look here, Hare," he says, dropping to

**"Come on, push!
The wedding's about to take place."**

the ground, "what *are* you doing?"

"Can't you see," says Hare, "I'm playing this," and he bangs a couple of little wooden hammers on the bottles in front of him.

Crow hops over, with a look of surprise.

"What's all this?"

"I haven't got a real organ, so the Mice helped me collect these bottles. I put water into them, more in some and less in others, so that every bottle makes a special sound. Listen! Isn't that beautiful! Clink! Clonk! Clo-clo-clo-Clonk! It's a wedding march. I wrote it myself. It's called 'Lots of Happiness, and a Long Life to the Bridal Couple.'"

"Splendid! But why a wedding march?"

"What! Don't you know that Blackbird gets married today? Ah! Here they come! Make way!"

Of course, everyone has remembered that it's the Blackbirds' wedding day. All the woodland folk are dressed in their best clothes and they line the path as the bridal procession arrives. Black Rat is Master of Ceremonies. The groom is wearing black and the bride has a beautiful delicate train that the Bumblebees are holding off the ground. The Mice have scattered perfumed flowers on the path, Hare is playing his music and the Blue Tits are singing in chorus:

May you both be very happy
And get from life the best,
Big fat juicy worms aplenty,
Bouncing babies in the nest.

Caterpillar watches from his leaf and wonders, "What should I do? Go down and join the procession or watch from here? Should I go to the reception or just have my usual lettuce snack? Oh, well, I'll decide, by and by . . ."

There is, however, one solemn face and glistening eye in all the general cheerfulness. It's Crow, standing to one side and looking sad. He always did have a soft spot in his heart for Blackbird. Indeed, he was once on the point of asking her to marry him, and now . . .

"Oh, well! For every Blackbird lost, there are a hundred others!" he exclaims at last, and off he goes gloomily into the wood.

The wedding lunch is laid out on a long table in the open air. The table is so long that no cloth could be found to cover it. Or rather, there is a big enough tablecloth, belonging to the Mouse Sisters, but they didn't want to use it.

"It's going to be used," they said, "only when we get married," which means never, because they are so perfectly happy together.

It took five tablecloths to cover the table, but it looks pretty and jolly too. And the woods ring with laughter and merriness.

Just as dusk is falling, along comes Caterpillar, very very slowly. But he has arrived too late! Everyone has left the table. There's not even a crumb! The Ants have carried them all away!

**Black Rat stands up: "I propose a toast.
Here's to the happy couple!"**

# Oak Tree Terrace

Everyone knew it would happen one day.

"I tell you," said Squirrel, "that it's nearly hollow. In fact, it *is* hollow. It can't stand upright much longer."

"That's right! That's right!" agreed the Bumblebees.

"Do you know how old it is? Nine hundred, maybe a thousand years old. It's the oldest tree in the wood. Poor thing, it will fall, sooner or later!"

They all heaved a sigh and gazed sadly at the great old rugged oak, which no longer bore acorns and was bare of leaves.

Then, one stormy night, a creaking sound was heard and a great crash.

The next day, everyone gathers in the glade round the huge uprooted oak.

"Its acorns were so tasty!" sighs Hedgehog.

"It was such fun playing hide-and-seek among the leaves and branches," says Blackbird.

"What a pity it's no use to anyone now," chorus the three Mouse Sisters.

However, Beaver puts on his glasses and, scratching his chin, says:

"Just a minute! Who says it's no use any more? Let me take a few measurements!"

Out come pencil and paper, and measuring tape. He bustles round the trunk, frowning. Then he exclaims:

"Now, if we take away some wood here, raise a wall there, cut a few windows and some doorways . . . it'll make a marvelous den! Den! It'll make a . . . an entire row of houses!"

A moment of stunned silence. Then Tortoise murmurs:

"That may be so, but who's going to do the work?"

"That's easy! The Woodpeckers!"

An agreement was drawn up in no time at all, in exchange for a bag of acorns. Then the Woodpeckers start to bore into the wood with their strong beaks, following Beaver's instructions. A window is made here, and a door there. In the meantime, Hedgehog,

**"NO! The doorway should be wider!"**

Oak Tree
Terrace

Mole and Badger are busy building the walls and making the window and door frames. A few days later, the big tree trunk has been converted into . . . yes, into a terrace of five little houses, which the Mouse Sisters sweep, clean and dust till spotless, and then put up the curtains.

The entrances are made, and there is even a balcony for hanging out the washing. Nothing like it has ever been seen before in the wood.

Then comes the day for moving in. Shrew goes to live at Number 1, the Hedgehogs at Number 2, Black Rat at Number 3 (and the first thing he does is set up the old grandfather clock his first wife left him). Hamster sets up house at Number 4 and Mole is supposed to go into Number 5, but . . .

"I'm not sure that I'll like it in there," he says.

"What! You won't like it?" exclaims Beaver.

"It's not that . . . You see, my hobby is digging tunnels. I wake up at night and start digging, and every now and again I stick my head up outside to see where I am. I couldn't dig tunnels in the terrace, could I? I might pop up in Black Rat's bedroom!"

"Oh, that would never do," Beaver agrees. "Listen! You can go underground and live in the cellars. You can dig all the tunnels you want there!"

"Now, that's a good idea!" says Mole, and he sets to work straight away. Before nightfall, he's very tired, but there he is, happy in his new home.

The tenants of Oak Tree Terrace peer in the window.

"It's just as well," they whisper, "that he's sleeping in the cellar! Listen to him snoring! He'd have kept us all wide awake!"

And so, the old oak tree, now stripped of its leaves and acorns, is still part of the wood.

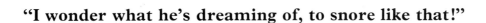

**"I wonder what he's dreaming of, to snore like that!"**

"That's the Plow," says Black Rat, "and that's Sagittarius."

# Shooting Stars

Black Rat is certainly the greatest adventurer amongst the woodland folk. He has traveled a lot and seen the world. As a youngster, he went to sea on a merchant ship (in the hold, of course, or rather, in the ship's kitchens, where all the food was). He never stops talking about it.

"How on earth did you see the world," asks Bear Cub, "if you spent the time shut up in the hold?"

"Aha, my lad! At night, when there was nobody around, I went on deck and saw the sea. And the sky. And the shooting stars."

"Shooting stars? What do you mean by shooting stars?" everyone inquires curiously.

Black Rat stretches out his paws. "What! Don't you know the stars shoot across the sky in summer?"

Hedgehog turns doubtfully to old Owl who, as everyone is aware, knows the skies and the night better than most.

"I say, Owl, is that true? Or is Black Rat pulling our legs?"

"Oh, it's true right enough. The stars do shoot across the sky. I've seen them myself."

"Of course they do!" exclaims Black Rat. "And tonight's the 10th of August, when there are even more shooting stars. Come along, folks, let's go!"

"Go where?"

"To the big glade, where we can see the sky! Ah! It's a wonderful sight! Come on, hurry!"

Bursting with enthusiasm, they all troop off behind Owl and Black Rat, who keeps talking about Cassiopeia, Andromeda, the Pleiades, and using other awfully difficult words. The Mouse Sisters travel on a cart Badger pulls, then come the others: the Frogs, Mole, Grasshopper. The whole crowd, in other words. Everyone is full of energy, though the Tortoises complain.

"Hey," they grumble, "you'll leave us behind if you go so quickly!"

Dormouse scurries on for a bit, but then he begins to feel sleepy. He starts to yawn, walks on with his eyes shut, bumps into a few trees, and as soon as he hears a voice say, "We're there," he

heaves a deep sigh, lies down in the grass and begins to snore.

Which really is a pity. For over the heads of the woodland dwellers, the dome of green branches has given way to an immense stretch of sky, like beautiful black velvet, sprinkled with sparkling stars.

". . . and that's the Plow," Owl and Black Rat say, "that's Sagittarius, and that one . . ."

"Oh! Look! A shooting star!" someone cries. Far up in the sky they see a streak of darting silver that appears, only to vanish from sight.

"There's another! And another one! Look!"

"Whoever sees the most can go home in the cart!" proclaims Owl.

This leads to a competition, and everyone stares upwards. Each time a star darts across the sky, it is greeted with cries of amazement and wonder, and every creature tries to be the first to call out.

Zzzz-zzz – Dormouse continues to snore.

"Do you know what we're going to do to this sleepyhead!" says Frog. "We'll play the wolf trick on him! Shall we?"

They all agree, so they tiptoe round the sleeping Dormouse and, at a signal, start to shout:

"The wolf! The wolf!"

Dormouse sits up with a frightened start, eyes wide and mouth open.

Everyone laughs.

"What a horrid trick!" sulks Dormouse. But the others just laugh and turn away to look at the sky again.

The hours go by and lots of stars shoot across the sky. Then come the first chilly shivers. The stars are fading, their light has gone and it is now very dark.

"How will we find the way back?" ask the Mouse Sisters.

"Leave it to us!" say Frog and Hedgehog.

They open a large basket and out swarm a hundred fireflies, which light up the path.

The woodland folk set off home by the light of the fireflies, while Dormouse, who is fast asleep again, happily snores on.

And Black Rat and Owl roll up the chart of the skies they had brought with them.

**"Be careful! It's such an old chart it might tear!"**

20

# The Swimming Pool

Yes, that was a very nasty moment!

It was a scorching day, the water in the stream was slipping by so coolly, and one of the Mice dived in. But just as he sliced through the air, he suddenly remembered he couldn't swim.

"Oh, goodness! What shall I do now?" he said to himself.

Too late! Splash! He was in the water. And the current would have swept him away, if Hedgehog had not appeared on the scene.

"Here, hang on to this!" he yelled, holding out a flower stalk.

Mouse grabbed the stalk and was pulled to dry land, frightened and shuddering with the cold. By sheer luck, a dreadful accident had been avoided.

The woodland folk don't want things like that happening a second time.

"We're not all like Otter, Beaver and Frog, who are at home in the water! Something must be done, now that summer's here, if we are to stop folk drowning!"

"It's quite simple," says Beaver, "we'll build a swimming pool!" Bringing out pencil and paper, ruler and compasses, he begins to do sums. Then he says, "Right! Off to work! Start digging here!"

"Here! In this field? But there's no water here!"

"Just start digging! Do you or don't you want a pool?"

"OH, YES!"

"All right, then! To work!"

They dig three holes in the ground, each a different depth, and each separated from the others by a bank. A little canal carries water from the

**"Grab this stalk!
And don't open your mouth
or you'll swallow the water!"**

stream into the holes and turns them into proper pools.

"Hooray!" cry the woodland folk. "Now we've got swimming pools!"

"Be careful, though," warns Beaver, "for the moment we're only going to use the middle one. In you all go, there's no need to be frightened."

It's a great day for everyone. Frog quickly builds a diving board, while Blackbird turns his nest into a boat and takes two Mouse Sisters for a sail. The third sister stays on the bank with the lifebelt, just in case! Otter has fun swimming underwater, then capsizing the tin can that Frog is using as a boat.

"Look out! Here's the fastest legs on skis!" shrieks Black Beetle, water skiing on a pod pulled by the Bumble-bees.

"Get out of the way! I'm going to dive!" yells another Frog.

"What chaos!" sighs Black Rat, taking it easy under the beach umbrella.

In the meantime, the Ants have arrived with their nutshell boat, and Caterpillar, ever kind-hearted, allows himself to be used as a gangway, while Hamster has discovered that Tortoise's tummy makes a very comfortable craft.

Beaver has not stopped for a second, and with the help of Hedgehog and his assistant, he is measuring the depth of the pools.

"Phew!" he splutters, spitting water, "this one is really deep! It's for only the best swimmers . . . Oh! Isn't that Cricket ever going to stop singing!"

Frog is organizing swimming classes. "I was watching you," he says to the Mice. "You were wearing caps, but you lack style. You swim like . . . well, like mice, that's all. Look! There are different strokes. There's the breast stroke, the back stroke and the butterfly . . . each has its own style, you see. But remember, lads, breathing is the important thing in swimming, and being careful."

Now they can really begin enjoying the summer!

**"You're a Frog, swimming's easy for you! We wouldn't mind being so good," say the Mice. "Nonsense!" exclaims Frog. "Why don't you try swimming the crawl?"**

breast stroke    crawl    back stroke    butterfly stroke

# The Corn Cob

"Look at this," says Ant number eleven (there are lots of Ants, you know, and each has a number). "Look what I've found!"

"It's only a kernel of corn," says Ant number thirteen.

"What's it for?"

"You can eat it if you want. Chop it in two, add some sugar or salt, and eat it. Like to try?"

"Yes, of course!"

The two Ants pick up the choppers and are about to split the kernel when a voice exclaims:

"Just a second! What do you think you're doing?"

It is Hedgehog, who stalks over looking very severe.

**"Be sure to give it plenty of water, then it will grow faster!"**

"We're going to eat a kernel of corn," the Ants reply.

"Silly things! Don't you know you can get an entire corn cob from this kernel? Bury it in the earth, water it, tend it, and after a while you'll find a cob with a hundred or two hundred kernels!"

"Really?"

"Definitely!"

The Ants whisper to each other for a moment, then turn back to Hedgehog.

"Listen," says Ant number eleven, "we'll give you this kernel and you plant it. If a cob does grow, give us half and keep the other half. How will that do?"

Hedgehog thinks it over for a second, then agrees:

"All right! Half each! It's a deal! Shake on it!"

Hedgehog buries the kernel, carefully spreading earth over it, gives it water and protects it from the strong sun and dew. After a while, a seedling appears. Filled with curiosity, all the woodland folk come to see it. And everyone has a remark to make about it.

"Gosh!" exclaims Mouse, "Hedgehog has worked very hard, yet he's going to have to share with the Ants, who haven't helped at all!"

"That's so, but the Ants provided the kernel, and without the kernel there wouldn't be a cob," retorts Squirrel.

"Craaw! Craaw! I say and repeat Craaw! There isn't going to be a

cob!'' caws Crow, shaking his head.

But Crow is wrong, for when the right time comes, a large plump softly bearded cob appears, its creamy color turning a golden red! And what excitement in the wood!

"We could have it with milk!" suggests Black Rat.

"No, fried!" says Frog.

"No, boiled!" urges Mole.

"No, raw!" says Beaver.

In the meantime, pencil and paper to hand, the Ants are counting the kernels. A hundred and seventy two! They shake hands with Hedgehog, then start taking their eighty-six kernels away to the anthill.

Hedgehog decides he'll have his kernels roasted and spiced with honey which the Bumblebees have brought. And it goes without saying that everyone is invited to the feast.

The fire is lit, the embers glow and the rest of the cob, smeared with honey, turns on the spit. What a mouthwatering smell wafts through the air! A tent is set up, and folk bring drinks. The only one not lending a hand is Crow. He flaps his wings impatiently.

"What are *you* doing?" Frog asks him.

"Me? I'm waiting for the food!"

There is plenty for everyone, and the roasted honeyed kernels are lovely and crunchy!

Of course, everyone would keep on eating if there was more food to be eaten, but then someone would have a sore tummy that night.

Which is exactly what happens to Mole, though luckily he has ripe juniper berries in the house, and these will cure any pain!

While lying in bed, waiting for his tummy ache to go away altogether, Mole hears a rustling noise outside and, looking out of the window, by the light of the moon he sees the Ants carrying away the huge cob, all gray and bare. Mole asks them:

"Hey! What are you doing with that?"

And the Ants, the eternal hoarders, reply:

"You never know when it might come in handy! We'll see what can be done with it."

**"Pull, Ants 1, 2, 5, 7 and 14! Heave away!" orders Ant 32.**
**"Why don't you get down and help instead**
**of giving orders!" grumbles Ant 5.**

# Fruit Punch

In the wood today there are . . . yellow leaves! The Mouse Sisters exclaim in chorus, "It's September!" And then again all together, "Blueberries! Raspberries! JAM!"

A moment later, out they pop carrying all sorts of baskets. They do this every year at the beginning of September, and with the help of their friends, pick the sweetly-scented tasty woodland fruits to make jam. And all morning, the sound of laughter and calling ring through the trees and among the bushes.

"Over here! Here! Look at all these, here!"

"This way! I've never seen raspberries like these before!"

"Run and see these blueberries!"

By lunchtime, every basket is full to the brim.

"Now who's going to help us make the jam?" the Mouse Sisters enquire. "Let's ask Tortoise . . ."

"Oh, not jam again! I can't eat jam any more! It makes me fat, don't you realize that? And I'll burst if I get fat! Can't you see how tight and stiff my coat is already? I was so fat last year I couldn't even get back into my shell and I caught one cold after another!"

"But we've a lot of fruit this year, and we can't throw it away! What'll we do?"

"I know! Make a huge fruit punch! I'll do everything! Don't you worry!"

And Tortoise, with Beaver's help, builds a strange device. To look at it, you'd take it for a seesaw, but if you examine it more closely, then you'll see it's a machine for crushing raspberries and blueberries.

"There, you see! The fruit is fed in here, you climb on to the seesaw, and it goes up and down. It's great fun, and it makes the fruit punch!"

The Mouse Sisters gape. "Ohhh!" they chorus. "It's wonderful!"

They set to work, though they're really playing a game too, and like all games, it has its own rules. Everyone that brings a basket of raspberries or blueberries wins the right to a bottle of punch and a turn on the seesaw. Anyone bringing two, gets two turns, and so on.

**"Who's going to help make the jam?"**

"Oh, we are much too light to work the seesaw," the Ants complain.

"Well, you can write the labels for the bottles!" say the Mouse Sisters. "Will you do that?"

And they do.

People are beginning to arrive from all directions. Along come the Bumble-bees, who haven't picked one berry, but want to count the blueberries (I wonder why?). Hedgehog and Beaver offer to be the tasters, and Grasshopper wanders about doing nothing, till he bumps into Cricket, who says:

"I'm not feeling too well today, I think I've caught the flu. But I've an idea this punch is good for me!"

Caterpillar is, in the meantime, dithering as usual, and peeps out of his mushroom home.

"What should I do? Go down or stay where I am? I'm not too keen on punch, but they're all having a jolly time. I could go on the seesaw . . . No, I'd become giddy. Well, what shall I do? Go down or not?"

More baskets of berries arrive, and the Tortoises, Hamster, Frog, Water Rat and the others amuse themselves taking turns on the seesaw. Each time the plank goes down, more punch flows into the tub. In the meantime, the Mouse Sisters prepare the bottles.

Finally, as the sun is setting rosily in the sky, and the first evening shadows begin to stretch over the wood, the fruit punch has been made, and the Mouse Sisters are putting the corked bottles in the pantry.

"Tortoise certainly had a clever idea!" they say in unison. "Crowds of people will be coming to visit us this winter for a sip of squash. Just wait and see!"

In the meantime, Caterpillar has at last made up his mind. "Oh, well," he says, "I'll go down!" But when he comes down from his mushroom, he gets a surprise, for all the work has been done, the fun is over, and everyone has gone home!

**"Let's not tell anyone where we've put them, or that greedy
Mole will give in to temptation!"**

# The Giant Wooden Clog

Yes, of course, a swimming pool is a very fine thing, but it's even more fun bathing in the stream. You have to be a really good swimmer, though. You need to be able to swim on the surface and underwater too, dive, swim down to the bottom, then shoot up and bob out of the water . . .

"Oh, dear! My poor head!"

As he floated up to the surface after a dive, Frog banged his head against something caught in the reeds and grass beside the bank of the stream. He has given his head a nasty knock! "I saw stars, I did!" he exclaims to himself. Then he takes a look at the object which gave him his bump.

"Well, I never!" he says. "What's this? A wooden clog! And such a large one!"

**"Let's use it as a boat!"**

Word spreads in a flash, and bursting with curiosity, and not a little alarmed, the woodland folk run to see it. Fox cautiously gets into the clog, peers at it and sniffs carefully.

"Yes," he concludes, getting out, "there's no doubt about it. There's been a foot in here."

"Whoever would have such big feet?" asks Bear.

"This is rather scary," murmurs Rabbit.

"There's nothing to be afraid of!" exclaims Beaver. "This clog may have had a foot in it at one time, but it hasn't now. That means it's ours. And do you know what we are going to do with it?"

"What?"

"Use it as a boat, to cruise up and down the stream, as far as the pond. Come on folks!"

We know the woodland folk very well by now, and we know too that when there's work to be done, they're always willing. So they busily set to work in all sorts of ways. The Woodpeckers bore the portholes and the hatch, the Mice make the curtain rails, the Mouse Sisters embroider the woodland flag with a fine mushroom for a crest. In other words, the wooden clog quickly becomes a proper boat.

"If it doesn't have a lifeboat, it's not a proper boat," says Black Rat who's an expert on boats, so the Grasshoppers

make a little lifeboat which bobs along behind. Then it's time to go aboard. Some folk, however, including Weasel and Grasshopper, simply refuse.

"You don't know what you're missing!" exclaims Tortoise. "Come on!"

"I'm scared," says Weasel.

"Scared of what? The water?"

"No!"

"Of the boat?"

"No, not that either."

"Of what, then?"

"I don't know. Sorry! I probably would enjoy it really, but . . ."

Cricket starts to gently strum "The Wooden Clog Song," written specially for the occasion. Bear and Marmot, the strongest, begin to haul the boat, and it plows its way upstream, amidst great applause. In the water, Otter keeps an eye on the hull. It really is splendid to see the clog sail on the sparkling water!

And they're all enjoying themselves on board. It's fun doing your traveling like that, with no effort! The Mouse Sisters chorus:

"Isn't cruising wonderful!"

Of course, you can hardly expect Bear and Marmot to keep on hauling the boat. It's only fair to give them a chance to sail too. But how will the boat go if they stop pulling?

That's where the Frogs come in. They invent an amazing contraption: a propeller worked by a special pulley system, with two folk pedaling to make it move!

From then on, the *Giant Clog* (the name of the boat) can travel without being pulled. Bear and Marmot, needless to say, are very pleased.

And yet, between cruises, one or other of the woodland folk sometimes wonders, "Who's the owner of such an enormous clog?"

**"Are you sure this propeller's going to work?
Shouldn't we take along a couple of oars, just in case?"**

# A Strange Picnic

Sooner or later, all the inhabitants of the wood get invited to tea and cakes at the Mouse Sisters' house (hmm . . . the perfect excuse for a scrumptious tea without anyone being able to call you greedy!)

On this occasion, the Mouse Sisters have baked a really gorgeous cake from a splendid mixture of sugar, maize flour, baking powder, vanilla and eggs! Naturally the three sisters decide to invite some guests, but this time they don't want folk like Black Rat and Tortoise, who are greedy and gobble everything so quickly. So they invite the tiniest and daintiest of the woodland dwellers: the Ladybirds, Cricket, the Grasshoppers, the Bumblebees and the Ants, as well as the Mouse nieces and nephews. And as it's a beautifully sunny day, they decide to have a picnic in the bluebell field.

The tablecloths are spread and the plates laid. The Mouse Sisters are busily putting out the slices of cake and glasses of blueberry and raspberry punch when the sun vanishes and a sudden wind begins to blow. Everyone stares upwards: the bright blue sky is now full of black clouds. A storm is coming.

"Oh, our picnic!" groan the Mouse Sisters.

Just then, Frog, Mole and Hedgehog appear in the bluebell field, out for a stroll. When they see the Mouse Sisters and their guests trying to hurriedly pack the tablecloths, plates, glasses and cake back into the baskets, they ask:

"What's happened?"

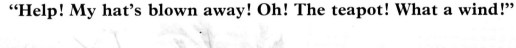

**"Help! My hat's blown away! Oh! The teapot! What a wind!"**

"Oh! We arranged a picnic, but this horrid weather is going to spoil it!"

"Don't worry! We know what you can do, don't we, lads?" says Frog. Mole and Hedgehog agree:

"Of course! Pick up your belongings. Don't forget the cake! And follow us!"

As the wind blows harder and harder, everyone troops after Frog, Mole and Hedgehog across the bluebell field, till they reach a corner where two bottles and a jar are lying among the grass and flowers.

"There you are! You'll find shelter inside!" says Frog.

"What a splendid idea!" exclaim the Mouse Sisters, while the Ants waste no time in bringing up ladders so that they too can climb into the bottles. And as soon as they're inside, Cricket and the Ladybirds realize they can slide down the neck of the bottles! Yes, the woodland folk will always find a way of having fun!

Cricket begins to sing, and even though the wind is howling and the sky becoming darker and darker, they're all comfortable inside the bottles and the jar, and the picnic is in full swing.

"You've really earned a reward!" the Mouse Sisters tell Frog, Mole and Hedgehog. Each is given a large slice of cake, and so is Black Rat, who just happened to be strolling by!

Next day, the Ants have a bright idea.

"Listen!" says Ant thirty-nine. "Why don't we use these bottles as greenhouses?"

"What are greenhouses?" asks Ant number seventy-five.

"They protect things that are growing, like flowers and vegetables, from the wind and rain. We could sow all kinds of seeds in them, in all seasons."

And from that day on, in the bottles-turned-greenhouses, the Ants grew all sorts of flowers and vegetables.

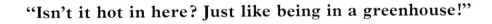

**"Isn't it hot in here? Just like being in a greenhouse!"**

35

# The Greedy Quail

It was a fine May morning when the sound of fluttering wings came louder and louder from the sky, and a little later, from the woodland glades came the noisy chirping of birds. Everyone, naturally, knew what this meant.

"The Quails! The Quails have come back!"

They had indeed! They had returned after spending the winter months in far-off lands where it is always hot. There! Another flock was arriving, and a fine sight it was too! Hundreds of quails flew past, dipping their wings in greeting, landed on the ground and immediately began to search for their old nests. The woodland would be all the more cheerful for their arrival.

It was lovely to see them pattering about searching for seeds and grains to eat.

But there was one quail who was not too keen on grain and seeds. He preferred buns and cakes, especially the ones the Mouse Sisters baked. This quail was known as Thumper, for he was large and plump, and each time he landed he came down with a thump, instead of with a soft gentle rustle the way his companions did.

Thumper was a really jolly bird, nevertheless. He would tell of his adventures on his travels, describe the lands he had seen and the dangers he had to face. He did this so well it was fun to listen.

"Once, in Africa," he would say, "I saw a hunter aiming at me! I ducked, the shot passed a fraction of an inch from my head! I ducked again, and as I did so, saw I was about to be swallowed by a snake! So I took to my wings, the snake reared up to grab me, the hunter fired his gun again. And would you believe it! That was the time a hunter shot a snake instead of a quail!"

It was so amusing to listen to Thumper that everyone outdid his neighbor in inviting him to lunch or tea. And after a while, Thumper grew so fat that when the first traces of mist and the early autumn colors appeared, and the other quails were getting ready to leave . . . well, he was so large he couldn't get

**"Your friends are starting to leave!"**

**"Look! The Quails are coming! I wonder if Thumper's with them?"**

off the ground. He tried and tried: he stretched his wings, he flapped them, rose a few feet into the air, then thumped right back to earth on his fat tummy!

What was he to do? He couldn't possibly delay leaving. He might run into a storm over the sea! He simply had to go NOW! So what was to be done?

Everyone thought about it, then Black Rat, clapping his paw to his forehead, exclaimed:

"I know! I remember once seeing a kite land in a field. It was lovely and it flew beautifully! I remember sketching it. Wait, I'll dash off and get the picture. I won't be a minute!"

A few minutes later, Black Rat returned, and the woodland folk, who had understood the idea, set to work straight away. They pulled here, stitched there, stuck this and trimmed that, and with everyone's help, especially the efforts of the Ants and Bumblebees, a kite was built.

"What are you going to do?" asked Thumper, somewhat alarmed.

"Tie you to the kite, and your sisters will pull you across the sky to Africa!"

"Oh, I'm so scared! I've never been on a kite!"

"We know that, but the cold weather's on its way and you can't stay here. You'd need to starve yourself for a week at least if you want to fly!"

"Starve for a week! Never!" declared Thumper. And a little later, there he was, tied to the kite.

It was not easy to raise it from the ground, but with the aid of the Bumblebees and the wind it finally soared into the air carrying Thumper, while the other quails got ready to pull.

"Goodbye, and thank you so much!" shouted Thumper. "See you next year! Have some nice cakes ready!"

The quails flew steadily away, till the kite was nothing but a white figure in the sky.

"Poor Thumper!" said the Mouse Sisters. "What kind of trip will he have?"

"He'll be all right," said Beaver. "The African animals will give him a great welcome. But unless they make him another kite to come back with, I'm afraid we'll never see Thumper again!"

38

# The Fawns' Overcoats

What a lot of snow! Such an enormous amount! It snowed for a whole week, and the wood is now white and silent. The birds are sheltering in their nests and some creatures, like Dormouse, Badger and Squirrel, have shut themselves up in their homes and, wrapped in blankets, have gone into hibernation, that deep sleep which lasts till Spring.

For them, the cold white season is a lovely time, and it is for the Mouse Sisters too. They don't hibernate, but in the warmth of home, they keep themselves busy, making the house even nicer and more comfortable than it already is. They polish the furniture, bottle fruit, knit vests and jumpers and embroider the sheets. This year, they're making a fine carpet for the living room floor.

They rarely venture out, except to fetch some flour, or a little honey for the woodland folk's favorite cakes. And to get some honey, one of the three Mouse Sisters, well muffled up, goes across the wood to see Woodcock. He gives her a lovely pot of golden honey he got as a gift from the Bees, in exchange for a can of sunflower seeds.

She is on her way home when she hears someone sadly sighing. She looks round and notices two little fawns beside a bush, shivering with cold. Winter may be fine for the hibernating creatures or for the Mouse Sisters, but not for deer and fawns, which must stay out in the cold and find barely anything to eat. For the snow buries the grass, and the bushes are all bare. Cold and hunger are dreadful things! Hunger can be satisfied somehow, because you can find a little grass if you scrape the snow away with your hoof, but there's nothing you can do to keep out the cold.

**"Come into the wood and ask for the Mouse Sisters. We'll see what we can do for you."**

And that is why the two little fawns are sighing and shivering.

"Oh!" says Mouse, feeling so sorry for them, and holding out some honey, "take this, it'll give you some strength!"

The fawns lick the honey and look at Mouse gratefully.

"I haven't anything else to give you now," she says, "but come into the wood. Ask for the Mouse Sisters – anybody will show you where we live. My sisters and I will see what we can do to help."

When she arrives home, she tells her sisters about the fawns and by the end of her tale tears have sprung to the Mouse Sisters' eyes. What can they do to help?

"They're too big to come into the house. Otherwise they could stay with us till Spring."

"Yes, indeed! Yes, indeed!"

"You see, they're feeling the cold more than suffering from hunger!"

"I have an idea!"

"What?"

"Why don't we make the poor things an overcoat each, instead of making a living room carpet?"

"Overcoats for the fawns! What a wonderful idea!"

"Let's start now!"

The Sisters set to work. They undo the carpet and make two fine overcoats for the fawns, and a cap for the younger one. They've never had such an enjoyable winter.

A few days later, they hear a gentle tapping at the door. They open it and see a damp muzzle and two round eyes, gazing hopefully.

"Oh, you've arrived!" exclaim the Mouse Sisters. "Good! We've just finished!"

And shortly after, over the white snow in the wood moves something never seen before. What a pity Dormouse, Badger and Squirrel missed the sight! It was quite extraordinary! A pair of fawns, looking like colored chess boards, gamboling happily in the snow!

**"They're so warm, and gorgeous too," say the Fawns.**

# The Great Flood

Suddenly one night, a great roll of thunder rumbles in the sky. Some of the woodland folk are so sound asleep they never hear a thing. Others wake for a second, tuck themselves up in their blankets and go back to sleep. But some of them become wide awake and think, "Thunder! Just like April? Thunder like that so early in the year? But Spring's still a long way off!" Then they go to the door and peer up at the sky.

It is covered with dark clouds, with the pale moonlight filtering through. Then it starts to rain!

You can see instantly that this is no ordinary shower. In fact, it rains for three days. The earth is sodden and is soon under deep water.

"It can't last," say some folk. "It's bound to stop soon."

But it doesn't. It keeps on raining. The streams are swollen into rushing rivers, the ponds become lakes. The waters start to rise.

Mole is the first to abandon his house. "Gosh! I nearly drowned! Every room and all the tunnels are full of water!" he gasps as he climbs a tree.

"Things don't look too promising," grumbles Crow. "We'd better hold a meeting."

So the Great Council calls a general meeting, and even as the woodland folk discuss things anxiously, the rain still pelts down. The water is already lapping at the doors of the houses.

"We must build a big raft and stay on it till the rain stops," says Squirrel.

But Beaver says, "No. It's too late. We haven't time to build one."

"What's to be done then?" ask the

**"Take Granny's old trunk too! And don't forget my knitting!"**

Mouse Sisters anxiously.

"We must split into groups, and each group must find itself a boat. We will have to go away from here."

"Where shall we go?"

"Towards the hills, where we'll be safe from the water. Come along, folks!"

The houses are evacuated in the pelting rain, and in what is now a flood, and each group finds itself some kind of boat. The Ants have their walnut shell, the Mouse Sisters a nest given to them as a present by Blackbird. Hamster climbs on to Tortoise, Grasshopper and the Ladybirds get into an old tin can. All the Frogs need is a log, but other woodland folk build sturdy little rafts, as you can see. With some friends, Snail has a paper boat, the Hedgehogs a tin can, and Otter pushes a matchbox carrying the Mice, and Dormouse wearing a life belt round his waist.

It really is a migration. Certainly everyone feels rather scared and very sad, of course, for they are leaving their homes. Cricket, however, tries to cheer the creatures up with the guitar.

The birds fly on ahead.

"On we go! Row for your lives!"

So on and on they sail, and the rain which had been pouring down stops at long last. Everyone heaves a sigh of relief, and when Badger shouts, "Hey, folks! Look up there!" everyone's gaze turns upwards, and they see that the thick clouds, which had hidden the blue sky for days and days, are beginning to part, and a faint ray of sunshine is peeping through!

"Hooray! The nasty weather has gone! Hooray!"

Yes, the worst is over. But . . .

But where are our friends now? They are safe amongst the trees, bushes and reeds, in another part of the forest. It is dark! Black Rat is staring at the horizon. Suddenly he leaps to his feet:

"It can't be! Take a look! Do you see what I see?"

"Gracious, yes! It's incredible!" gasp the Mouse Sisters.

Black Rat can scarcely believe his eyes. He has seen something that is very strange indeed. BUT WHAT IS IT?

What it is, we shall find out in the next book.

**"I thought I saw a boat slip past, with a strange figure wearing a big hat at the oars!"**

# Titles in this series

Heron

Ants    Ducklings    Ducks

Fawns    Cricket    Lamb

Cuckoo    Caterpillar

Ladybird    Bumblebee    Black Beetle    Blue Tits